This book belongs to
my friend:

_____

A NOTE TO PARENTS

Ask most children what they think a hero is, and they will probably describe a person who uses supernatural powers to help rid the world of large-scale terrible deeds and villains. In *Everyday Heroes*, Little Bill discovers that in fact, most heroes are regular people. He learns that he need not look any farther than his own neighborhood to witness heroic acts of kindness and giving.

As you and your child read *Everyday Heroes*, ask her to think about people she knows who have jobs—police officer, firefighter, teacher, and animal lover—like the characters featured in the story. Then encourage her to think of other people in the community who help others. Together, recall memories of when one of these heroes played a part in your family's life.

Involve your child in little acts of heroism toward others. For instance, help an elderly neighbor with a simple chore or bring soup to a sick friend. Acknowledge the generosity of time and effort that others contribute to your family. Also, teach your child from an early age to send thank you notes. It is never too early to learn how to give generously and receive gratefully.

Learning Fundamental: **social skills**

For more parent and kid-friendly activities, go to www.nickjr.com.

Everyday Heroes

Published by Scholastic Inc., 90 Old Sherman Turnpike, Danbury, CT 06816

ISBN 0-7172-6634-6

Printed in the U.S.A.

First Scholastic Printing, March 2003

Everyday Heroes

by
LaVonne Carlson

illustrated by
Dan Kanemoto

SCHOLASTIC INC.

New York   Toronto   London   Auckland   Sydney
Mexico City   New Delhi   Hong Kong   Buenos Aires

"Space Explorers to the rescue!" shouted Little Bill in his best Captain Brainstorm voice. "I need your help, Little Bill. We have to save the planet!"

"Sure, Captain Brainstorm. Super-fast hyperblast!"
Little Bill exclaimed. He lowered his invisible space
helmet and blasted into space.

"Little Bill, who are you talking to?" asked Little Bill's father from the hallway.

Little Bill giggled. "I was helping Captain Brainstorm save the world. That's what superheroes do."

"Do you think Captain Brainstorm would mind if you take a break?" Little Bill's father asked. "I'm going to Uncle Al's store, and I would like your super-company."

"Sure, Dad," said Little Bill. "I'll bring Captain
Brainstorm with me. He can be super-company, too."

"I feel super-lucky to have such super-company,"
Little Bill's father laughed.

Little Bill and his father began walking.
Suddenly a fire truck rushed past them and
stopped at the next corner.

"Captain Brainstorm, maybe we can help with the fire!" Little Bill said.

"Hello, Mrs. Brown. Where's the fire?" asked
Little Bill.

"Oh, there's no fire, Little Bill," Mrs. Brown replied.
"My parrot flew out the window and into that tree.
Now he's afraid to fly down, so this nice firefighter
is rescuing him."

When they got to the corner, the police officer was standing at the crosswalk.

Little Bill was confused. "Hello, officer. Did someone do something wrong?"

"I thought firefighters only fought fires," said Little Bill.

"Oh, they do lots of different things to help people," Mrs. Brown said. "They're real heroes."

"See that, Captain Brainstorm?" Little Bill said. "Firefighters are heroes, too."

Little Bill and his father started walking again.
"Look!" said Little Bill's father. "There's
someone else who helps people—a police officer."

Little Bill looked aroun[d]
expecting to see a police
officer chasing someone.

"I thought firefighters only fought fires," said Little Bill.

"Oh, they do lots of different things to help people," Mrs. Brown said. "They're real heroes."

"See that, Captain Brainstorm?" Little Bill said. "Firefighters are heroes, too."

Little Bill and his father started walking again.
"Look!" said Little Bill's father. "There's
someone else who helps people—a police officer."

Little Bill looked around,
expecting to see a police
officer chasing someone.

When they got to the corner, the police officer was standing at the crosswalk.

Little Bill was confused. "Hello, officer. Did someone do something wrong?"

"No," the police officer smiled. "The traffic
lights are broken, and there's a lot of traffic today.
I'm here to make sure it's safe to cross the street."

"So the police don't only protect us from bad guys?" Little Bill asked his father as they crossed the street.

"That's right, Little Bill," his father replied. "They do lots of other jobs to keep us safe."

"So even when they aren't chasing bad guys, police officers are heroes," Little Bill said.

"Absolutely!" agreed his father.

Soon Little Bill and his father came to the pet store.
"Here's my favorite place!" Little Bill said happily.
He always found something interesting in Percy
Mulch's pet shop window, so he peeked in to take a look.

"F-R-E-E," Little Bill spelled. "That spells FREE.
Why does that kitten have a sign that says FREE?"

"Let's go inside to find out. You can ask Mr. Mulch,"
his father suggested.

"Hello, Little Bill," said Mr. Mulch.

"Hello, Mr. Mulch. Why does that kitten have a sign that says FREE?" asked Little Bill.

"I found that little kitten. He was all alone and hungry. I have too many other animals to keep him, but I'm trying to find him a home."

"That's nice of you, Percy," said Little Bill's father.
"I guess you're his hero," Little Bill giggled.

As they left the pet store, Little Bill saw his teacher bending over someone on the sidewalk. "Hello, Miss Murray," he said, running up to her. "What are you doing?"

"Oh hello, Little Bill. I'm just fixing this girl's skate," Miss Murray replied.

The girl stood up. "That's perfect," she said. "Thank you for helping."

Little Bill turned to Miss Murray. "Yesterday, you helped Andrew and me learn to spell dinosaur. And today, you helped someone who isn't in our class. I guess you help lots of kids."

"That's true, Little Bill. Teachers like helping people. See you later," she called, waving good-bye.

"Miss Murray helps people learn all kinds of things," Little Bill said to his father. "I think that makes her a hero, too."

As they walked on, they heard someone calling from a window. It was Emmaline, a friend of Little Bill's great-grandmother.

"I'm so glad to see you," Emmaline said to Little Bill's father. "I've been wanting to thank you for fixing my front door. Now it opens and closes easily."

"You're welcome, Miss Emmaline," said Little Bill's father. "I'm glad I could help."

Little Bill looked up at his father. "Dad, are you a hero, too?" he wondered.

"What do you mean, Little Bill?" his father asked.

"Miss Emmaline was so happy that you helped her. I think you're her hero," said Little Bill.

"I just try to help people when I can," his father explained.

"I guess that's what heroes do," Little Bill said. He thought about all the times his father had helped him.

Soon they arrived at Uncle Al's store.

"Hello, Little Bill. How's Captain Brainstorm?" his uncle asked. "Are you still planning to be a superhero like him when you grow up?"

"Well, I do want to be a hero," said Little Bill. "But I want to be a real hero."

"Like a firefighter or police officer or teacher?" his father asked.

"No," Little Bill smiled, "a hero just like you!"